Standing Stones

Castle ruins

Norah's field

School

Dolly's field

Smiff's field

Zizz's field

Crow's Woods

For our parents,
Maud and Stewart Williams

Text copyright © Tom Allen
Illustrations copyright © Patsy Allen.

From an original idea by
Patsy Allen.

All rights reserved.

Licensed by Libba Jones Associates.

Cover design by D. Baxter.

Published by Peter Haddock Limited,
Bridlington, England.

Printed in England

Adventures of the Rainbow Scarecrows

ZIZZ CLEANS UP

by Tom & Patsy Allen

Dolly was picking herbs when she met the otters sitting on the river-bank looking glumly at the water.

"Why aren't you swimming?" she asked.

The otters pointed and Dolly saw for herself. The water, which was usually clear and clean, was cloudy and covered with bubbles and dirty foam.

"Whatever has happened?" she gasped.

"It's been like this for days," sighed one of the otters, and they shook their heads sadly.

"I wonder where it's coming from," murmured Dolly. "Don't worry, we'll sort this out," she added firmly.

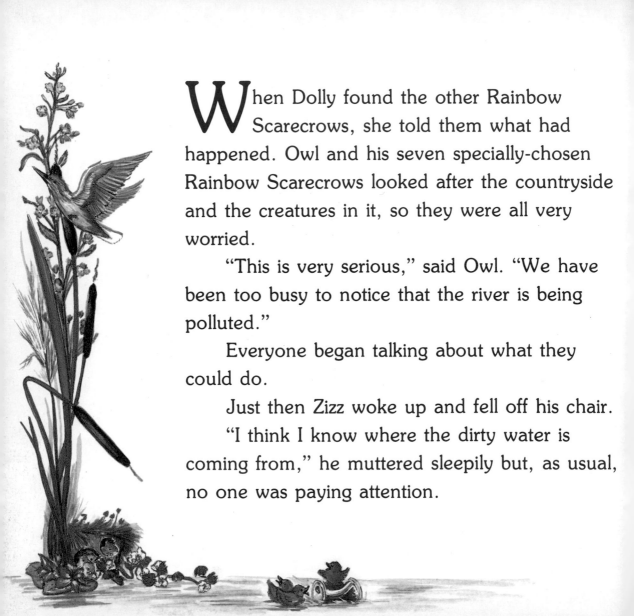

When Dolly found the other Rainbow Scarecrows, she told them what had happened. Owl and his seven specially-chosen Rainbow Scarecrows looked after the countryside and the creatures in it, so they were all very worried.

"This is very serious," said Owl. "We have been too busy to notice that the river is being polluted."

Everyone began talking about what they could do.

Just then Zizz woke up and fell off his chair.

"I think I know where the dirty water is coming from," he muttered sleepily but, as usual, no one was paying attention.

Humph," said Zizz to himself. "They think I don't know anything, just because I'm a bit dozy sometimes and I like a nap now and again. Well, if they won't listen, I'll have to do something about this on my own."

Next morning, Zizz went back to the riverside where he had enjoyed a quick snooze the day before. He saw that the water was dirty and grey, and the rushes on the bank yellow and wilted. Zizz followed the river until it brought him to the factory. He quickly saw what was wrong.

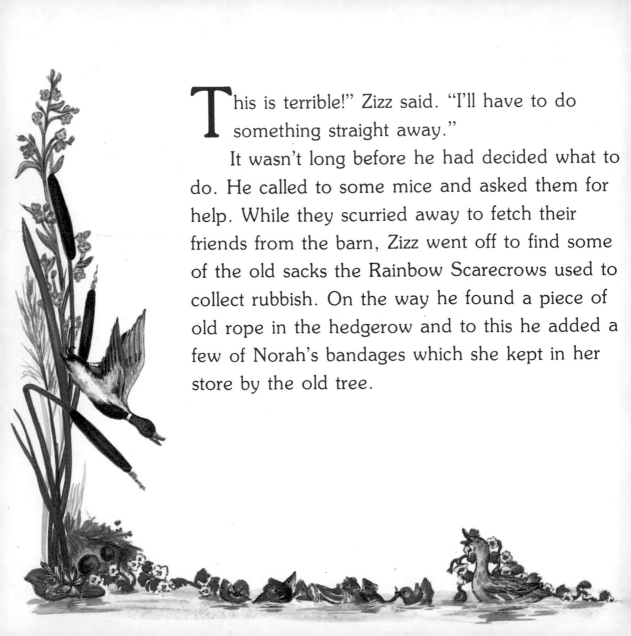

This is terrible!" Zizz said. "I'll have to do something straight away."

It wasn't long before he had decided what to do. He called to some mice and asked them for help. While they scurried away to fetch their friends from the barn, Zizz went off to find some of the old sacks the Rainbow Scarecrows used to collect rubbish. On the way he found a piece of old rope in the hedgerow and to this he added a few of Norah's bandages which she kept in her store by the old tree.

When Zizz got back to the river there was a huge crowd of animals waiting. In front of them was a big pile of twigs, leaves and sticks which Zizz had asked them to collect.

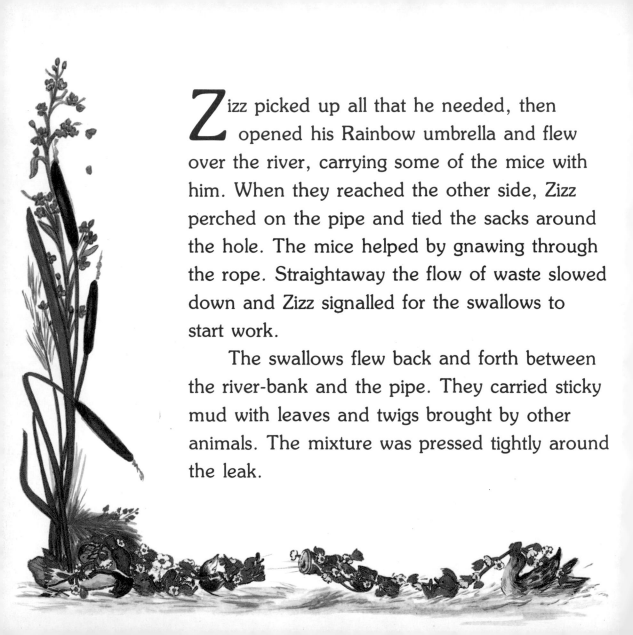

Zizz picked up all that he needed, then opened his Rainbow umbrella and flew over the river, carrying some of the mice with him. When they reached the other side, Zizz perched on the pipe and tied the sacks around the hole. The mice helped by gnawing through the rope. Straightaway the flow of waste slowed down and Zizz signalled for the swallows to start work.

The swallows flew back and forth between the river-bank and the pipe. They carried sticky mud with leaves and twigs brought by other animals. The mixture was pressed tightly around the leak.

At last the hole was completely filled in. The plan had worked.

"We won't have to worry about the river being spoiled any more. We've mended the pipe," shouted Zizz.

Everyone cheered and felt pleased.

Zizz set off to find Owl and the Rainbow Scarecrows in Acorn Woods. Everyone had heard from the swallows what Zizz had done.

"Well done, Zizz! You're not as sleepy as we thought!"

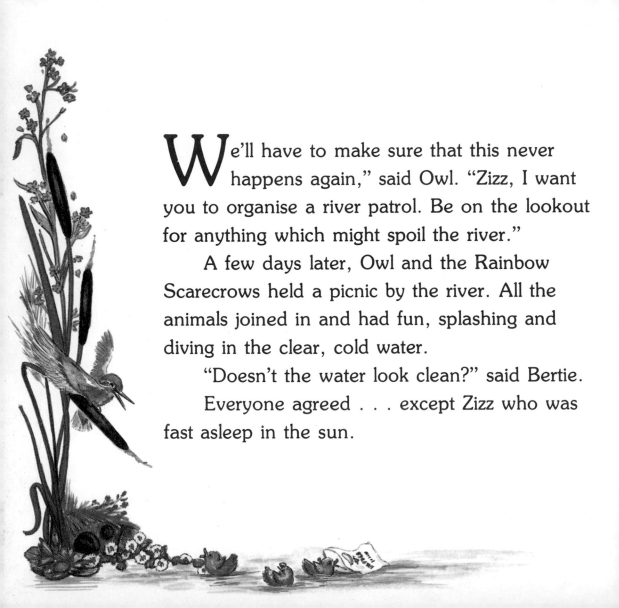

W e'll have to make sure that this never happens again," said Owl. "Zizz, I want you to organise a river patrol. Be on the lookout for anything which might spoil the river."

A few days later, Owl and the Rainbow Scarecrows held a picnic by the river. All the animals joined in and had fun, splashing and diving in the clear, cold water.

"Doesn't the water look clean?" said Bertie.

Everyone agreed . . . except Zizz who was fast asleep in the sun.

Owl's tree

Scruffy's field

Abbey ruins

Bertie's field

Poppy's field